Boy in the Darkness

by
Anne Schroeder

BOY IN THE DARKNESS BY ANNE SCHROEDER
Published by Trailblazer Western Fiction
an imprint of Lighthouse Publishing of the Carolinas
2333 Barton Oaks Dr., Raleigh, NC 27614

ISBN: 978-1-64526-056-1
Copyright © 2019 by Anne Schroeder
Cover design by Elaina Lee
Interior design by Karthick Srinivasan

Available in print from your local bookstore, online, or from the publisher at:
ShopLPC.com

For more information on this book and the author, visit:
https://anneschroederauthor.com

All rights reserved. Non-commercial interests may reproduce portions of this book without the express written permission of Lighthouse Publishing of the Carolinas, provided the text does not exceed 500 words. When reproducing text from this book, include the following credit line: "*Boy in the Darkness* by Anne Schroeder published by Lighthouse Publishing of the Carolinas. Used by permission."

Commercial interests: No part of this publication may be reproduced in any form, stored in a retrieval system, or transmitted in any form by any means—electronic, photocopy, recording, or otherwise—without prior written permission of the publisher, except as provided by the United States of America copyright law.

This is a work of fiction. Names, characters, and incidents are all products of the author's imagination or are used for fictional purposes. Any mentioned brand names, places, and trademarks remain the property of their respective owners, bear no association with the author or the publisher, and are used for fictional purposes only.

All Scripture quotations, unless otherwise indicated, are taken from the Holy Bible, New International Version®, NIV®. Copyright ©1973, 1978, 1984, 2011 by Biblica, Inc.™. Used by permission of Zondervan. All rights reserved worldwide. www.zondervan.com. "NIV" and "New International Version" are trademarks registered in the United States Patent and Trademark Office by Biblica, Inc.™

Brought to you by the creative team at Lighthouse Publishing of the Carolinas (LPCBooks.com): Eddie Jones, Shonda Savage, Jennifer Uhlarik, Sarah Hamaker, Brian Cross, Ann Knowles, and Jennifer Leo

Library of Congress Cataloging-in-Publication Data
Schroeder, Anne.
Boy in the Darkness / Anne Schroeder 1st ed.

Printed in the United States of America

Praise for *Boy In the Darkness*

Anne Schroeder is a writer who understands the importance of how minorities in the West have shaped America for what it is today. *Boy in the Darkness* is a stellar example of not only her copious research but her understanding of storytelling. She weaves a richness into her words that reflect the era and traditions of a Chinese boy who tumbled into a cave, and the voices of a female and flute that give him hope and courage. Schroeder's savvy choice of words and dialogue reflect the era and culture of both Chinese and Native American, and her story is a smooth three-strand tale woven into one descriptive legend.

~Carmen Peone
Award-winning author of *Girl Warrior*

A haunting tale of spiritual quest, physical suffering and the worth of a life. Fascinating detail with a perspective seldom heard from in tales of the old West.

~Sam Kaffine
Former wildland firefighter

A fine piece of writing and storytelling with a great twist at the end. The author's evocative prose lifts you to hope and dashes you to despair as indentured servant Man-Gee is trapped in a cave with a broken leg. He draws on the strength of his ancestors as he hopes to live, then resigns himself to his fate.

~Heidi Thomas
Award-winning author of the "*Cowgirl Dreams*" and "*American Dream*" series

Dedication

*To the unsung peoples who keep reinventing
the American West.*

Part One

The Shadow Boy

"Boy—*opschieten*! Make haste, you mangy mutt. Now!"

The boy was on his feet, searching the rolling land for a mottled Dairy Shorthorn cow with a rope around its neck before the Master finished yelling the few English words the boy understood. The harshness in the tone did not surprise him. Always the same—he must hurry. Already the camp bustled as men backed mules into their traces and slammed wooden boxes shut, and mothers gathered their children. So many duties on this trek to Oregon Territory, made worse because he was a worthless servant in this strange land. If only Grandfather were here, the boy could show everyone he was smart and willing. But in the noise and filth of the camps, there was no time to learn what the strange English words meant or how to use them himself. There was only time for Master's boot to kick his scrawny backside and for Master's voice to shout cruel words.

He had tried so many times to explain that his name, Man-Gee, was an honorable one. Grandfather said the name came from a saying, "Gee Sun Gee Meet," but the meaning made no sense: *To emerge from itself and perish of itself.* What significance was that for a boy at the brink of his manhood? To talk of perishing at such an age was foolish. His nature was happy; many times he laughed and sang with the other cowherds, even if they saw him as a person without wisdom. Grandfather explained that his name had a feeling of the Tao in it, profound and arcane secrets that would reveal themselves to him in time. His name, Man, meant *full*, but he could not recall a time when his belly was full. Surely his father had not consulted wise counselors when choosing his name.

But no matter. Master called him Mangy, like a dog with hair falling off in patches. And now his actions had brought dishonor on his head. Shameful. The weight hung like a heavy burden suspended from his walking stick, a gift Grandfather had carved for him at the time of their parting.

He pushed through the herd of weary beasts without seeing the animal he searched for. When he had sat down to rest after the wagon train stopped at noon, the cow had been grazing with the others. The animal had to be close by. Master would not be pleased if the milk cow was no longer with the herd. Milk was not to his liking; it tasted to him like animal blood smelled, hot and earthy, but the animal was worth at least three of him—Master impressed this with each lash of the ox-whip when a worthless servant such as he, Man-Gee, displeased him.

Man-Gee glanced up at a sky filling with soft buttermilk clouds that reminded him of the milking bucket he struggled to carry every morning and evening. No time for clouds. The prairie rolled in a vast sea of brown and grey shadows where only great eagles soaring overhead could find their way. He turned his head, searching above the waist-high sage, but no matter where he looked, emptiness claimed the land. He crouched and began running, trying not to wince as sagebrush tore his skinny ankles. Master had spoken. His offense this time would not be forgiven.

Seeing no place where a straw-colored animal might hide, he ran toward a nearby outcropping while his coarse black hair, with its budding queue cut short by Master's wife, covered his vision. He swiped it away as he zigzagged across the bushes with one eye out for rattlesnakes and the other for a mottled cow. His toes kicked up patches of dried dung that many wagon wheels had churned into fine dust, but this was of little concern. He covered his nose and mouth, and turned into the wind.

His heart pounded inside his skinny chest as he sprang toward the rock outcropping. Master had grabbed his uneaten scraps and flung them into the fire, but a missed meal was nothing compared to this trouble. A boy's five years of indenture would be doubled if he failed to return with Master's precious cow. Behind him, the wagon train began to move. He forgot his fear of snakes as he leaped from boulder to boulder, listening for a cow's bell. When he heard a faint tinkle ahead in the grass, his knees nearly buckled in relief. He sprinted across an open area, then spied the animal silhouetted against a rock.

Without warning, his legs pitched forward. The rim of earth crumbled. The bottom fell from under him, and he was swallowed by darkness.

Dank air sucked him downward while jagged rocks scraped his skin like the sting of a thousand scorpions. He landed with a crack of pain. Something hard pierced his side, and he felt his ribs pop. His lungs emptied. He fought to breathe, but his *chi* drained from his body; he could feel it flowing out with each tortured wheeze. He ceased fighting—for surely this was the death that fate had chosen for him—and with his acceptance, fortune smiled on him. Darkness claimed him, and the pain disappeared.

His first thought when he returned to the living was that he had been eaten by one of the monsters in Grandfather's tales. His head pounded, and each movement created a firebrand that no amount of screaming relieved. His arm flailed out and smacked against his walking stick that had followed him into the hole. He gripped the handle where Grandfather had carved a snake coiling around the smooth teak while fireworks exploded behind his eyes, brighter than the Chinese New Year celebrations to which Grandfather had taken him.

His nose caught the scent of blood, and his body recoiled with such terror that he began shaking uncontrollably. Clenching his aching ribs, he curled into a tight ball and began keening, *Help me, Grandfather. I am here in this place where a dragon waits to devour me. Let me escape with my life. Plead for me to the gods, please, Grandfather. Please, Father, Mother, make honorable request to the gods.* He could not remember the prayers for when a boy found himself in the grip of evil, but Grandfather knew this prayer and more. Grandfather would protect him. The ancestors would understand; it was not death he feared, it was the thought of living even ten minutes more.

The Divine Master was benevolent. Man-Gee once again faded from the world, and everything went dark again.

He awoke to hear voices, and his heart swelled in gratitude. Master had tracked the cow and had found his worthless servant. In his excitement, Man-Gee forgot about his leg until he moved, and his scream pierced the cave.

Voices filled the opening with cautious murmuring. Their language was not the guttural German that Master used with his family, or the broken English the family used with other immigrants; the murmurs filtering down were filled with grunts and long pauses. His nose detected the odor of campfires and unwashed bodies. He called up, pleading, but the only answer was a handful of pebbles that descended to pepper his head and body.

Grandfather has sent men to rescue me. I will show my gratitude.

He chanted prayers of thanksgiving, not caring that his high-pitched wailing was slurred and barely human, even to his ears. No humiliation would be too great if the gods would only favor him. Five more years of servitude would be welcome; fifty years he would gladly trade. Even his entire life would not be too steep a price to feel sunlight on his face once more.

Again and again he shrieked in his Mandarin tongue, but his pleads were ignored by the voices whispering above. He struck his walking stick against the cave walls until the pain of breathing caused him to drop it clattering on the ground. Suddenly the thin ray of sunlight was pierced by a shadow. His wailing broke off, and he squinted upward, every nerve focused on the thing being lowered into his pit. The opening was too small for a person, and the shadow was only a small item, but surely a means to pull him out. He lifted his good arm and waited.

A packet dropped, splashing cool liquid on him. His fingers felt something smooth and heavy like the intestines of dogs his mother cleaned before cooking—only much bigger than any dog's. It was a gut bag smelling of rancid animal. He grabbed it and squeezed foul-tasting water into his parched mouth, shutting out thoughts of everything but his thirst. Something else thudded to the ground beside him. He smelled the odor of meat, and his stomach roiled. He would wait for Master to pull him up.

Comforted by the water, he waited for the digging to begin. Instead, the sound of fading footsteps filled his ears.

"Come back," he wailed. "You come back for Man-Gee. I work hard for you. Do many labors. Not ever lose cow again. Promise. Promise. Promise . . . "

Minutes passed while his echoes filled the cave. His voice grew hoarse from screaming, and his eyes ached from gazing into the noonday sun. When silence thundered in his ears, realization hit him like a stone. Nothing was as he hoped. This harsh land offered only bad fortune and evil omens, nothing more. If only he had remained in Grandfather's wise counsel. But Grandfather was no longer among the earth. Man-Gee buried his head on his arm and wept as a small child does in his mother's arms. When his eyes emptied of their small river, wracking pain claimed his entire body. He gingerly probed his thigh and felt bare bone beneath his fingers.

He lay back, but the pain in his ribs cut off his breathing, and he shifted, wincing at each movement on the hard rock slab. His temples throbbed like someone had hung a temple gong between his ears, every stroke a fresh torment. When he could bear it no longer, he rolled onto his good hip and ran his hand across the parts of his body that he could stand to touch. His hip was bruised, his back and shoulders had scrapes and crusted blood. His ribs burned with fire, and every breath brought a wheezing sound from his chest.

He lay as still as a corpse and imagined his mother cradling him, whispering soft assurances. In this position he stifled a sob and clamped his eyes to shut out the pure and unbroken darkness.

***

Man-Gee drifted in and out of consciousness while the yang of the sun gave way to the yin of moonlight in the soft, feminine coolness of the cave. Each time, he woke shivering and stiff with pain—like a willow sapling, its trunk still alive even as its branches withered. He smelled the stench coming from his leg where death nibbled his *chi*. A furnace burned inside him, fed by each heartbeat until he struggled to shift positions on the damp, rocky ground. Sweating with exhaustion, he managed to move his hand a few inches. Fortune smiled. His fingers found the water bladder, and he pulled it close to spill a few drops on his swollen lips.

Night passed, replaced by thin rays of sunlight. Many hours later, the sun again gave way to a blanket of twinkling stars. The cave grew warm, then cooler. He drifted in and out of delirium where dragons and monsters filled the darkness, roaring and clawing at him until his fingers were covered with blood from his leg.

The sound of arguing woke him. In his fevered dream, the figure standing at the opening appeared hoary and threatening. It crouched on its belly with its head cutting off the sunlight, its red eyes gleaming in eagerness as it stared into the pit. He called to his tormentor, but his voice trembled with thirst and terror so that he sounded even less human than before. He increased his pleading, but the shadow figure retreated, and sunlight once again flooded the shaft. Something fell toward him, a ball of fire burning on the end of a stick. He watched while it sputtered and burned itself out. When the Voices hooted in laughter, he wished he had the strength to throw it back to show them that his pride was still strong.

A huge furry beast dropped like a dead bird, filling the cave with the musky stench of an animal. It landed so near that its fur touched him. He screamed and waited for it to spring upon him like a tiger, but it remained still. Above, in the sunshine, the Voices laughed at his terror. His fingers brushed the hair, and he forced himself to hold steady. A warrior would not cower waiting for death; a swift victory would bring him glory. His fingers gripped his stick, and he edged closer until he could feel the beast's heat, warm like the sun. Bravery rode his thin shoulders as he inched his hand to a place where matted fur gave way to softened skin. It was a tanned buffalo hide. Trembling, he let his stick clatter to the floor while he tugged the heavy rug over his chin, unashamed that tears clotted his eyes. Warmth crept into his toes and fingers.

"Grandfather, let this not be a dream," he pleaded.

Without moving, he fell asleep.

When he awoke, the odor in the cave told him that food was nearby. He groped about the floor until he found a tilted, overturned gourd that contained a lump of thick, glutinous stew. He pulled out a chunk of bison belly and popped it into his mouth, the meat cold, fatty, and more delicious than anything he had ever eaten. His fingertips found spilled bits of meat and broth, which he scooped into his fingers, draining the gravy, dirt and all. When his stomach rumbled and threatened to revolt from the heaviness of the meal, he lay still.

In his hunger he had not noticed that the Voices were gone and only an overhead cloud filled the opening.

Fury welled up inside him, anger as a Zú warrior might show to his enemy, but directed at himself for accepting his fate so willingly. He would not perish in this cave. In a burst of desperation, he propped himself against the dirt wall. He ignored the sweat burning his eyes and took hold of his leg below the break. Pain seared through him, and he bit his lip to keep focused. His broken ribs pressed into his side, and he struggled to stay conscious, even as darkness pulled him under. A scream echoed in the cave, startling him. He watched himself working, but his mind floated above him, lightheaded and detached. Finally, Grandfather's gods heard his prayer. He tugged his leg into place and felt the bone reconnect just below the knee.

Spasms rocked his body, and fireworks exploded behind his eyes. Sweat mixed with his tears. His hands shook so hard that he would scarcely pick up the deerskin thong, a gift from the Voices. His finger hooked it, and he managed to lay a gnawed animal rib against the torn flesh of his leg and lash the cord around three times. With a last tug, he secured a knot before he fainted.

He woke to thunder and only a dull, steady ache where a searing agony had been before A blinding shard of lightning momentarily lit up the cave, showing him for the first time the dimensions of his prison, a rounded cave as large as his grandmother's hut back home in Chanchow with smooth, straight walls. But no place for him to gain a foothold to climb out after his leg healed more. Each time the lightning flashed, he studied his surroundings to see if monsters hid in the crevices, but each time he saw nothing. Soon rainwater began to trickle into the opening. He thrust his empty gourd under the biggest drops and rolled to the side to stay dry while the storm raged above him.

Sleep came hours later, with a hazy, restless dream in which Master cracked the ox-whip his backside with such force that the sky broke apart. He chased a cow, but each time he caught up to the creature, it disappeared. Again and again he searched, but no matter how hard he tried, it stayed just out of reach. His mother appeared, smiling and gesturing. When Master dragged him away before he could reach her, his pleading brought no change in her expression. Instead, a huge bear rose up from the darkness and wrapped its claws around his throat.

Man-Gee woke, kicking and clawing. In time, his heart slowed its frantic thumping and his sobs subsided. He lay still, covered in his own sweat as a coyote pack called out above him. He heard sniffing and saw two beady eyes staring down the hole.

"Get out of my sight!" he shouted in a shrill Mandarin voice, his tongue thick and dry so that the words sounded like an animal caught in a trap. A moment later the eyes disappeared.

He waited for sleep to reclaim him. His parched throat tried a song that his mother had crooned, but the words sounded raspy and the effort hurt. He remembered the coo of doves, the sounds of scratching hens on the path to the rice field, the rooting of pigs in the yards, the sounds of laughter coming from the huts. He dreamed of his grandmother and the tea she made. Her face was hard to recall, but he saw her, stooped and delicate, with her tiny, bound feet and her brightly colored robes, her eyes, snapping and alert, pleased that he remembered a poem exactly as she had recited it to him. He could almost taste the almond cookies she kept in a small wooden box and the tiny cups of tea she made especially for him.

Daylight filtered into the opening, and with it, the sound of digging.

"Man-Gee is down here," he called. "Down here." He ducked his head when a dirt clod fell, nearly landing on the water gourd. He pushed the container to safety and called again, "Down here." An animal growled menacingly in response. He found his stick and cracked it against the rocks, bringing a sharp pain to his ribs.

"Get away. Go now." he hollered, beating against the wall without caring that his precious water splashed onto the floor. "Go. Get out of my sight." How many times had he heard those same words shouted at him as he ran down alleys, fleeing to escape angry merchants with a bowl of stolen rice hidden under his arm? Now he yelled with the same ferocity.

He discovered the intruder's identity when the musky odor of skunk filtered into his cavern. This time his rage was real, his shrieks menacing. The skunk casually took its leave, but not before leaving its calling card imbued in his nose, his robe and even his water.

***

Man-Gee's days in the cave passed with the speed of a dead turtle. His body twitched with fever. His breath came in slow, labored wheezes. His body ached all the way to his toes. His face grew hot and his tongue swelled. The sun crossed the sky while he lay suspended in a dreamlike stupor, his gaze focused on a beckoning light as he waited to die.

In that altered state, his mind played tricks on him. He was again on the boat from China where the days passed slowly, the sun hot and heavy and the dank quarters filled with stench and decay. He saw again the men and boys stripped to their small cloths or naked, and heard the floors creak when the sailors walked on the decks overhead. He felt the ship strain and buckle when the sea tossed it about, playing with it as if it were a toy. Crowded into the hold, he waited impatiently each day for one of the sailors to open the hatch and to throw a bucket or two of sea water onto those who were lucky enough to sit close. He learned to listen for the sound of the hasp being lifted in order to be the one beneath the cooling water. When the water splashed on him, it was if the ocean called to him, telling him to be patient.

The lightning that illuminated his cave for three nights in a row brought back the memory of being trapped in the boat, so many people that he often couldn't move. Now he longed to feel the press of people next to him. When a bolt flashed directly overhead, a tiger crouched along the opposite wall. He waited for it to pounce, certain that death waited beyond its shining fangs, but the tiger chose to spare him that night. It leaped onto a lightning bolt and rode through the sky, with fire showering the earth as it disappeared.

Man-Gee dreamed of his mother, the quiet, lovely woman who devoted her waking hours to him until the time his father left to search for work in a distant city. When Grandfather died, he moved with his mother into a small shelter, upstairs from where old men smoked long pipes and stared without blinking. Often, when Man-Gee had tried to sleep, he heard the grunts and moans of animals beyond the canvas partition that separated his mother's sleeping mat from his own. She had warned him never to move from his mat once he was put in for the night, and he was careful to obey. Always in the morning the noise was gone, but a musky, unpleasant odor, unlike her dainty person, filled the small space. When she woke, she would air her bedding and sprinkle her floor with the fresh laurel and mint they gathered together on the banks of a creek.

Again and again, his dreams returned to the ship. In his mind he sat with his legs folded beneath him, trying to keep his breathing still. He practiced meditating to avoid the repugnant smells. Happiness flooded his body when a bucket of gruel, containing bits of chicken like his mother made, was lowered into the hold. He would hold the liquid in his mouth and make believe it was the rice his father harvested in the flooded fields that Grandfather had planted.

In the cave, he gathered his coarse, filthy hair with its short queue, and imagined the day when he would be a man with a braid to his knees. He dreamed of the fluffy rice in his mother's bowl. When he woke, he was chewing the ends of his hair.

On days when his brain burned with fire, he remembered what life had been like before his father left. It was a game he had played as a very young boy, when he tried to block out the sounds behind his mother's partition. Now, once again he was helpless, a prisoner to sounds, but this time he had a warm bed. A fine buffalo robe. Sometimes he dreamed that he was swimming with Grandfather's water buffalo in the Wide River.

One night, Grandfather came to him in a dream. Man-Gee pleaded for him to help, but Grandfather only smiled. "The four realms are within your thinking. Sickness comes from illusion. If you want to do away with it, you will need to believe in other than that which is inside you."

"How will I know who this wise person is that I might recognize him? Is it Master?" His question amused his Grandfather, who again smiled.

"When you find him, you don't recognize him. When you recognize him, you don't see him. Do not rely on appearances, and he will come. Or maybe it is not he, but she. You can't be sure." With those words, Grandfather disappeared, but his words kept Man-Gee awake until the first light.

He made excuses for his delayed rescue. Perhaps Master had fallen ill and must recuperate before hauling him out of his hole. Perhaps the cow had been injured and could not travel quickly. Many were the reasons he gave for the delay, but the offerings of food and water from others gave him hope. When his leg healed, he would be lifted back into the light, and he would recognize the miasmas of the Tai as Grandfather had taught.

A poem flittered into his mind—one his grandmother had recited as they picked fruit from the heavy plum tree that shaded the gate of their cottage flittered into his mind. He had laughed at the time, thinking the words were meant for him, for he loved his grandmother. But she told him that the words came from Confucius himself. In the long hours of evening, the words returned to him.

> Plop fall the plums; but there are still seven.
> Let those gentlemen that would court me
> Come while it is lucky!
>
> Plop fall the plums; there are still three,
> Let any gentleman that would court me
> Come before it is too late!
>
> Plop fall the plums; in shallow baskets we lay them,
> Any gentleman who would court me
> Had better speak while there is time.

***

The days seemed to stall in the yang season of summer heat. The sun cast its light from the south like a ferocious tiger, seeking to reach into the bottom of the cave. The Voices did not come for many days. No longer did the rains drip into his drinking gourd. He learned to sip sparingly, and even then he suffered from thirst. The grass above turned brittle and dry, snapping and crunching when creatures crept near. The scent of sagebrush and buffalo grass drifted into the opening, and the summer sun heated the cave until Man-Gee lay on his robe, tossing from side to side, his mood restless and irritable.

No longer did lightning fill the sky with a thousand bursts of fireworks. At midday, the sun bored into his cavern until he was forced to shift positions. Once he tried looking into the sun, but his eyes hurt for many days afterward. He felt his fingernails growing longer, like the merchants who sat motionless, each with one finger crooking a pipe while they studied the comings and goings of the peasants with half-closed eyes. Like theirs, his fingernails grew long from a life of idleness. Grandfather would say he was a worthless boy.

When his ribs eased, he dragged himself along the floor of the cave, feeling the walls for a way of escape. Near the ground he found a spot where the rock gave way to crumbling mud. His fingers began to dig, gouging into the soil, for surely there was an opening that had allowed the cavern to form. He lay on his belly until mud covered his hands and arms, but his hard work was rewarded with only a tiny bit of moisture trickling from a fissure. Still, each drip was like the song of a lark in his grandmother's village, a source of water for days when the Voices failed to come. He grew stronger, braver, more determined. His good humor returned.

One hot evening, when the breeze blew across the grasses and the night birds had yet begun their flights, a silent Voice visited. For long moments he waited to hear grunts or coarse laughter, but no words were spoken, nor did his nose detect the smell of an unwashed body. Instead, the scent of sage grew heavy. A sprig of sage landed next to him, filling the cave with a sweet, wild scent. Slowly, a strange new sound filled the air, the sound such as that made by cranes flying overhead; sweet notes from a flute until the pure sound was replaced by a girl's laughter, croaked and dry as though she had not heard her happy voice in many moons. Then the music began again, the notes gaining strength as if the girl took courage from the song. For many minutes she played while Man-Gee lay on his rug, twirling the sage in his fingers and imagining the girl. He recalled his grandmother's poem about the lover who waited with plums dropping down.

The night birds called, and the music ended.

The next night she was back, this time with a skin of water. He tugged on the thong, and the girl laughed and pulled the rope back a bit before he managed to pour the water into his gourd. Then the rope disappeared into the sky. When she began playing again, the flute's song meandered like a bird's warble, twisting and bouncing until it became a secret language between them. He imagined the girl with dark eyes and blue-black hair, and he wondered if they would meet again when he was no longer on the earth.

A new thought came to him, something Grandfather had taught him in a story about a great philosopher. A talking skull had brought the man wisdom. "Among the dead," the skull told the philosopher, "none is king, none is subject. None is Master. There is no division of the seasons; for us the whole world is spring, the whole world is autumn. No monarch on his throne has joy greater than ours."

Tonight, he was a king. The music heated his blood and made him feel that he was no longer alone. The girl's tenderness flowed from the notes into his ears, and his body felt free and light. He recalled a promise once made. "Do not let death find you until you have earned the love of a good woman," his grandmother had implored him. He had made the promise, unsure of how he might keep his word. Tonight, in the beauty of the flute's whispering, he imagined that the girl's light hand touched his brow and his heart had responded.

He lay still long after the music ended, and the night grew silent in the emptiness of the girl's leaving.

***

Man-Gee nibbled a piece of flat bread that tasted strange to his tongue, but the nutty flavor satisfied his hunger. Master's wife had placed small balls of dough in a black pan made of iron, so heavy that it took all Man-Gee's strength to lug it to the river and scrub it with sand when supper was finished. When the lid was lifted each night in a cloud of steam, the small white dough appeared like mushrooms, dense and steaming. Before he washed the heavy pan, he would stick his head inside and run his tongue along the cast iron to taste the salty remains.

He chewed a piece of meat slowly so that it made juice in his mouth. The meat was tough and stringy, but he learned to pull the meat fibers loose with his fingers before putting them into his mouth. One day he bit into a scrap of bread and felt a sting. He ran his finger inside his mouth and found a hole where his tooth had been. Under the shaft of light, he saw the tooth standing upright on the bread like an egret in a rice field. There was no help for it; he pushed the tooth back into its space, holding it until the sun's light disappeared into yin nighttime, and still it refused to rejoin the other teeth. He felt the hole where the tooth had been and wondered if he were destined to be toothless like the ancient men in his village. With sad heart, he rolled the tooth into a square of soft hide and laid it beside his other treasures.

Many times, his belly roared from hunger by the time the offerings of meat and water rained down from above. But he conditioned his unworthy self to expect nothing, so that his gratitude would be greater when gifts appeared from the sky. Grandfather would be pleased. But secretly, fear filled his entire body that the Voices would abandon him. His fingers scratched out a place in the cavern where a thin line of water squeezed from a crevice in the rocks. On days when his throat grew parched with waiting, he pulled himself to the wall and licked the moisture from the rock wall.

On a listless day, he threw the rib he had been gnawing against the wall. It landed with a rattle on a growing pile of other bones, and the sound startled him. His night soil lay unburied, and the cave held the stench of many days. His hair itched. His mother's soft remonstrance sounded in his ear. "My son, you should honor the place where your body slumbers." His cave was filling with filth, a reminder that he had failed to heed his mother's teachings.

Inching along on his good hip, he gathered everything that littered his cave, laying the bones in a neat pile and the skins and gourd, the leather thong and his deerskin shirt in a high place along the wall. He buried the night soil. His favorite possession was a sharp rock that fit his palm, something Master called an arrowhead. He had seen one impaled in the chest of a white man on the wagon train, and the man had died. Perhaps it was a death rock. He wrapped it carefully in the packet along with his tooth. Perhaps when he was released he would find the meaning to such mysteries, for his tooth had died as surely as the man with the death rock in his heart.

When the overhead sun blazed into the hole, Man-Gee unwrapped his leg. He put his scant weight on his good leg, hoping that he could stand, but the pain was unbearable. The muscle felt shriveled and knotted when he ran his hand below the break. The wound was raw, worse than the wounds on his back after Master's whippings, the flesh ulcerated and hot to the touch.

He willed himself to stand until sweat poured from his brow and his leg trembled with pain. Exhausted from the effort, he sank onto his blanket and considered how he would need his leg to work. Celestials were required to dig ditches and do the hardest jobs in the settlements. Without his leg, he would be cast aside to die with the starving dogs. Worse than starving, a girl would not choose to marry a man with a withered, useless leg.

Fever burned inside him, so that hunger no longer troubled him, but his body craved the sweet water. He satisfied his thirst with the seepage from the rocks and from the meager gut bags of tepid water that arrived sometimes just before he thought he surely must perish from thirst.

The girl came only in the black nights. He waited for her in the nights of the waxing moon, but the moon grew round and began waning to a thin crescent before she came again when the sky was dark and the moon hiding. She arrived just in time, for the tiger of death had waited many nights at his side. He imagined how it would be to sit beside the girl, watching as she played her flute. In his mind he was a warrior and she his maiden, wooing with music that spoke a love song. But it was a man's place to woo. He should play music for her. Work for her. Live for her.

In the days of the waxing moon, delirium slept in his head while the tiger kept watch. He spent every waking moment patiently kneading his muscles, pressing the flesh until he could scarcely endure the pain. But he did not stop. He rolled his walking stick up and down the leg, breaking the stiffness while he tried to recall his grandmother's poems. Master's children had been teaching him the few English words they knew, and he practiced as he hauled harnesses and water, and scrubbed pots. Now he wished he could remember the words his Chinese ear heard, but his tongue found many of the sounds impossibly strange. He had learned to speak the name his master had given him, "mane-gee-mutt." Master would always call his worthless servant by this name while resting near the wagon wheel with his bottle of whiskey beside him. Many times, he opened his worthless eyes to see Master's stout boot swinging toward him in the darkness. When it was over, he would stare at the bright fire, trying to absorb his pain, and wish that he had a thick pair of boots like Master. Now he thought about what the skull had said: No master, no servant.

The nights the girl did not come, he lay silently, listening to hear her approach in the grass, but the yin of the moon grew from a thin crescent into a full moon and waned again before she came again on a dark night. He called out, but his words seemed to confuse her, and the music stopped so he remained silent. He wondered if this new feeling was love, the kind that his mother held for his father. He began carving statues for her from the animal bones that littered his cave, using the arrowhead to make delicate faces, wings, and legs. One night he managed to toss a small carved horse straight up. Unlike most of the others, this one did not fall back down to break on the rocks at his feet. He heard her pick it up and exclaim in her light, sweet voice. He heard her soft giggle and the sounds of her hands tying something to the deerskin rope. Soon she lowered it, and he felt the flute in his hands. He had no opportunity to react before she retreated as quietly as she had come.

In the darkness, his fingers felt the soft wood with five finger holes carved in a straight row down the middle. Two thin deerskin strips were tied below the last hole. The end was carved into a crane's head allowing the sound to come out of the beak. The wood smelled of cedar, clean and fresh. He placed the end against his lips and blew a sharp, quick note that sounded more like a croak than the beautiful sounds she played. He took a breath and tried again, and this time one of the notes sounded better. Over and over he blew until the sounds began to be beautiful. He remembered the tune she played, and he practiced it while the moon drifted overhead and the sun rose the next morning. Finally, holding the flute like a bride, he fell asleep.

She came again, surprising him on a night when the moon was full; he recognized the sound of her soft moccasins while he was preparing to practice. He took a breath and released it slowly into the reed, careful that his fingers were in the correct position. The first notes were shaky, but his heart knew the way of the notes, even if his fingers did not. He played his love, his loneliness, and his desire to walk beside her and to hunt for her. His music told of his understanding that she, too, was lonely, a slave captured from a warring tribe and forced to serve hard masters who beat her across the back with a piece of firewood when she was slow. He played his understanding that she was scarred and branded, mutilated like himself, but that she contained a heart that was true and beautiful, and his for as long as the sun shone. Everything he felt: his longing, his hopes and dreams were there in his music, as though the Divine Master understood.

The moon was high overhead when he felt a need to halt to take a drink of water from a gut bag two children had dropped into his eager hands while they clapped in glee, as though feeding a pet animal. From above, he heard a rushing of moccasins and the sound of a man's angry words. He heard the slap of hands and the slave girl's scream of pain before she was dragged off into the grass. He heard her screaming her love into the air, her voice defiant, not scared, and then the night was silent once more.

He felt old and tired, and more useless than ever in his life. "*Hao tie bu da ding, hao ren bu dang bing*," he shouted and heard his words echo back to him. "Good iron is not used to make nails. Good men do not become soldiers." He was good only for scoffing, no warrior. "I am a fool, and I will die here." He pounded the rock with his flute, over and over, until the wood snapped in two pieces, one jagged edge catching his shoulder and drawing blood, but the pain was nothing compared to what he felt inside. Afterwards, he gathered the broken parts of the flute and clutched them to his side while he wept bitter tears.

He felt himself falling into a long, deep hole worse than the one he was trapped in, for this time he was alone.

***

Man-Gee lay listlessly, trying to breathe, but the cave was awash in melancholy. The air seemed thick and filled with a scent like the cook-fires of the wagon train. It was hard to breathe. If he tried to inhale, the smoky air choked his lungs. He shifted so that he could see the sky and heard a far-off roar like the hurricane winds that swept through his old village. The earth shook, increasing until it seemed like a wagon train rolled over the top of him. Of course it was a wagon train. Hadn't he seen with his own unworthy eyes the trains that stretched across the horizon? A wagon master could surely lead his people this way. Perhaps word had come down the line that a servant boy was missing—how could it be otherwise? When he was rescued, he would find the slave girl, and they would escape together.

"Down here. Down here. It is me, Man-Gee."

He stood on his good leg and called upward, expecting at any moment to see a floppy-eared mule nuzzling around the opening. Dust clouds distorted the sun, and he could hear the wheezing breath of animals laboring past. As he stared into the light, a bit of dirt fell into his eye, and he slid away from the opening, blinking rapidly. But it was not oxen that passed. He caught a glimpse of a shaggy beast jumping over his opening. It was a huge buffalo, and then another, and then so many others that he grew weak waiting for one to step into the hole and come crushing down on top of him.

Dust filtered into his cavern, and he dragged his pelt against the wall, searching for pockets of air while his ribs wracked with the effort of coughing. Once in a while he would hear a break in the thunder, and he would relax, thinking surely the herd had passed, but the ground would start shaking again and another group would fill his cavern with its dust.

He thought of Grandfather's abacus. If he had one, he could count the bodies that thundered over him, something to pass the time. Instead, he lay sweating under his pelt—waiting. The sun must have descended, but it was hard to tell because dust shadowed the land. However, he could no longer see the dark bodies leaping, so he assumed it was night. But the vibrations continued.

He woke to see something swaying back and forth like the leather thong that held his water gourd, but alive. A serpent. Terror pumped through his veins. He had seen enough rattlesnakes on the trail that he had no doubt that it was trying to escape the thundering hooves. Too afraid to move, he watched as it dropped to the floor and disappeared into the darkness with a sound of loose rattles like those on the bands the men of the Dragon Dance wore on their ankles.

The thundering was gone. He kept his eyes fixed on the spot where the snake disappeared until his attention was caught by a strange, acrid smell drifting into the enclosure while he fought for every breath and thought he would die from lack of air. Choking, he groped for the water gourd and snatched it up, drinking deeply until the smoke drove him into his rug. He could barely breathe, and his throat felt scratchy from fear as much as from the snapping sounds of sage bushes exploding from the fire. He burrowed beneath the pelt, forgetting even the snake as he listened to fire devour the grass where he had searched for his cow. Overhead, smoke dimmed the light of the sun, and the late morning was as dark as dusk.

Heat made the rug unbearable. He crawled out and lay on the cool rock, sucking in the fresh air that was trapped near the ground. From the recesses he heard a rattle as if the snake, too, sought air.

Fingers of red flame caught the grass at the opening, and a blazing twig fell onto the floor. He watched hypnotically as it burned itself out in a spiral of smoke and another twig joined it. Then the cave was alive with burning embers as if all the fireworks in his grandmother's village had been lit at the same moment, shooting up and sideways and sparking each other.

Gradually, the last ember faded. Man-Gee sat listening for the snake in the darkness, regretting that he hadn't hunted the serpent while the cave was brightly lit. For a long shining of the sun he waited for the snake to strike, but when he heard it searching for food, his anger reminded him he wasn't ready to die yet. A plan formed in his head. Without hesitating, he reached for his walking stick and beat the ground like hunters in his village when they rousted tigers. He felt for a thin rib bone he was carving into a pagoda and tied his arrowhead to the tip with a scrap of leather, like a lance. He wadded a scrap of deerskin and laid it in the center of the light circle, grateful that the serpent hadn't chosen to sun itself yet this day. Biting his lip to keep from crying out, he pulled himself up on his good leg and practiced throwing the lance at the target. The sun continued across the sky while its shadow grew from a thin crescent to quarter moon in the light circle. The sun seemed to stall in the sky. At the pace the floor circle filled, it would be hours before the sun was overhead. With the lance at his side, he lay on his pelt and waited.

The sun was overhead when he awoke from a restless dream, aware that danger lurked nearby. Terror bolted him upright, and he saw the snake warming itself in the circle of light. Stealthily, his fingers closed over the crude lance. Curling his good leg beneath him, he made ready to prove himself as a warrior. Grandfather would expect this of him.

When his breath settled, he slipped from the rug and slowly rose onto his good knee, biting off the pain as he fought to stay conscious. Deliberately, he took aim and threw. The lance flew straight. Man-Gee watched the snake fighting death, its rattles scraping from side to side in a desperate attempt to free itself. He ended its life with his stick and used the arrowhead to slice off the rattles. Afterwards, he tied them to his good ankle like the dragon dancers in the street festivals. He smiled at the way they bounced and crackled when he shook his foot. He would have music now. His own voice had become a lonely sound.

His stomach growled, and he realized he hadn't eaten in several suns. Swiftly, he pulled the skin loose and tore at the snake flesh. He pulled a strip of meat and placed it on his tongue, surprised that it tasted like the bantam hens that ate bugs in Grandfather's yard. It had been a long time since he tasted chicken, and this was good. When his stomach no longer rumbled, he set the rest aside. Tomorrow's meal would not be as moist, but he would not go hungry. Beyond that, he had no way of knowing.

The fire marked a change in his resolve. For many days, no Voices had come with food or water. He gave thanks for the tiny stream that seeped through the fissure, clearly a gift from Grandfather, for it fed a warrior's heart. He played the broken flute, the part that still held three unbroken holes, but his heart ached with regret. The shattered instrument was a reminder of what he had lost: the music—his battle sound. Cursing himself for a fool, he realized that his rescuers were no longer coming. There was no escape except through the shaft from which he had fallen; better to die trying to escape than to continue living like a pet cobra waiting to be fed a fat rat.

He worked quickly, not sure whether his actions were real or the result of his delirium, for he could smell the festering poisons, feel the heat flowing through his blood, spreading death to every part of his body. Fever fueled his resolve, for the death tiger waited impatiently. He lined his possessions in a row: his walking stick, several sturdy bones that he had carved into shapes, knotted deerskin rope, a horsehair rope, a roasting stick that had come with a piece of meat, his arrowhead, rug, and a water gourd. There was little that he could use to climb up. Easing back on his bed, he considered the weight of Grandfather's walking stick. It could hold his weight, maybe. He tied the rope onto the stick and knotted it in two places; if he was to climb the rope, he would need knots where his feet could rest. Getting the stick lodged over the hole would be the hardest part, but he was a warrior. After all, hadn't he killed a snake? His aim would not fail him.

For the rest of the day he practiced throwing the stick to the entrance of the cave, aiming for the small opening at the top. Finally, he rested when his ribs burned with heat and his body trembled with hunger and exhaustion. His prayer to Grandfather was for fresh meat to build his strength.

***

Man-Gee stared as the small wolf fell noiselessly into his hole, thinking this was another nightmare until it landed beside him, an inquisitive pup that had spent the morning sniffing at the opening until it lost its footing and fell. It lay stunned on the rocky floor. He quickly finished the kill before his heart softened; a pet would ease his loneliness, but he had no food or enough water even for himself.

He gave thanks for the gift of fresh meat and began skinning the pup with the arrowhead that had been sharpened to a knife-edge. Famished, he tore out the heart and bit into it, wincing at the pain in his teeth. How many days it had been since he had eaten, he could not tell. He slowed when he felt his stomach protest, taking smaller bites and chewing carefully without wasting any part. Grandfather would not approve of wasted meat.

He needed something to cover himself once he escaped. His shirt and trousers were worn to rags from sliding along the rough ground, and his bare rump was abraded from sitting for days on the rocks. He replaced them with a breechcloth that he made from the wolfskin.

The meat from the wolf imbued him with its strength and cunning. Fresh from a night of sleep, sated and determined, he leaned against the wall, propping himself with his strong leg while he took aim at the slit of earth far above him. The sun's energy was too powerful, and the contest was unfair, but each toss taught him a new lesson. In his excitement, the pain in his leg disappeared, replaced by courage and determination. When his belly demanded food, he ate more of the meat and felt it feeding his muscles. In the early afternoon he gathered his energy and crouched almost to the ground. Springing upward on his good leg, he launched the stick through the air, straight up to the sun. He watched without moving as the stick sailed through the lip of the opening and failed to return to his hand. Luck walked beside him this day. Man-Gee gave the rope a tentative tug and saw that it held. He tugged more determinedly and still it held. With all the courage he possessed, he grabbed onto the rope and suspended his weight. Still it held. Relief flooded his body, and he sank to his knees in disbelief.

While he rested, he formed a plan. Once free, he would need his belongings, his buffalo rug especially, but the weight of it would be great. Still, he had to think of afterwards. The climb would be difficult for him alone, but what point was there to escape if only to die of exposure?

He would fit through the opening better if he was naked, or almost so. He removed his worn shirt and stuffed it into the gourd, carefully placing the arrowhead inside for safe keeping.

He finished the last of the meat and drained his water before he lay down to rest his throbbing leg. The pain had returned since his triumphant throw, but he had no time for such concerns. Instead, he glanced around the cave. Part of him was reluctant to leave, but such a small part that the call of freedom was loud, like a bird's trill. With a mighty breath, he grasped the rope and began to pull himself up.

He made it, hand over hand, to the height of a cherry sapling before he felt himself sliding back down. The climb would be more difficult because his feet could not grasp the rope. Each time he tried, pain from his weak leg sent spears through him. He rubbed dirt onto his hands and tried again. Again, he slid back. He had seen many men and boys climb the high trees of his grandmother's province, gripping the trunk like monkeys, but each time he tried, his stiff leg refused to bend.

He found his arrowhead and began cutting a thick hide strip that he used to lash his legs together. This time he managed to make it almost halfway before one of the hide strips slid over his knee and fell to the floor. Disgusted, he felt himself slipping to join it. Bruised and blistered, he knew that his hands would not make many more attempts; by now he was covered in sweat, his injured leg throbbing. Tears filled his eyes while he slumped against the rug and allowed sleep to take the edge off his misery.

When he awoke, the sky opening was pitch-black, the cave so dark that he couldn't tell up from down. Something was squeezing his leg—another snake? His body screamed in terror until he realized how much he welcomed death. He felt his thigh and discovered that the strip was still attached. His sweat had stiffened the hide; it had dried attached to him like a second skin. Hope kindled inside him as he located the other strip and used his own urine to moisten it before tying it as tightly as he dared. Then he lay back and waited for it to dry and shrink.

***

He drifted away from himself into a troubling dream where a strange, ethereal light filled the sky with streaks of coral, a lucky sign. In his vision, he pulled his body upright and rubbed his hands in the dirt, grimacing as he took the rope into his blistered hands. He had taken the time to cut fingerholes into small squares of deerskin, and he used them like crude gloves to alleviate the pain. Gripping the rope between his knees, he inched himself slowly upward. By the time he reached the first knot, his hands were a solid mass of pain, but he bit his lip to keep from crying out and forced himself upward. Soon he reached the second knot. His right shoulder burned with a searing pain that made it almost useless. Transferring his weight to his other shoulder, he continued up.

Suddenly he felt a blast of direct sunlight on the top of his head, so intense that it burned his scalp. Sunlight seared his eyes. He fought to keep them open while tears ran from the corners of his stubby eyelashes. His nose reached the opening, and he squinted enough to see that the earth was scorched from the wildfire. His body was skinny, but even so he barely fit through the opening. Slowly, like an inchworm, he pulled himself up, chest, waist, buttocks, and hip until, with a mighty effort, he pulled his injured leg from the hole. He collapsed onto his back and lay staring at the sky where a single cloud waved from the faraway mountains. Still squinting in the early sunlight, he saw the place where the Voices must have knelt. He rolled from the opening and saw a line of trees where a shallow creek ran with pure, cool water. A doe and fawn stood on the other side, cautiously watching until they returned to the sweet young grass that had grown after the fire.

He struggled to his feet and turned in a slow circle, seeing a distant line of wagons, followed by herds of cattle and horses. It was close enough that he knew Master was not among them; he had only to see the dust from their journey, and to hear the laughter and cursing to know that he would be safe. He saw the rock outcropping where a mottled cow stood. Clumps of sage dotted the gently rolling plains, its new sprouts hiding fat sage hens and jackrabbits. A herd of antelope raced across a vast, shallow lake that shimmied in the sunshine.

Then a sight more beautiful than all the others. An Indian girl ran toward him, her arms outstretched in greeting. She was beautiful in spite of the slave tattoos, her eyes soft and wise, her hair flowing loosely around her shoulders. But it was her smile that captured him, a smile of such joy that he understood; he was her lost warrior who had returned from battle.

***

When he awakened, betrayal struck at his heart. His eyes opened to darkness. He lay motionless, trying to understand how his body could still be wrapped in the stinking skin, and the air around him dank and sunless. Reality dawned with a force that crushed his breath inside his lungs. A dream. The freedom was an illusion, nothing more.

Wracking sobs tore at his insides, sending shards of fire into his body from the wound. He didn't want it to be his fate to die in this putrid hole, with shame for a life poorly lived.

When his desolation and anger faded, he remembered the lessons Grandfather had sent these many days and nights, and he felt shame because he desired to bind himself to this life and not to the plan of the Creator. He heard again Grandfather's words: *Life is given because the time is right. You will lose it because the order of things passes on.* Today was the time for neither sorrow nor joy, but time to accept the process of change. The yin and the yang were not to be refused. Grandfather had told him the Creator would care for him. Man-Gee would sleep now, and later he would wake, and it would be all right.

He worked quickly, building an altar to honor his ancestors with tiny pagodas and fish he had carved by feel in the darkness. He buried his night soil. He collected his ropes and deerskin thongs, rolling them neatly together. Although his throat ached with thirst, he reached to where water dripped from the fissure and smashed the opening with a rock, sealing the entrance lest he should fail in his resolve. Slowly, the trickle of water became a growing ball of mud, the pure water lost to him forever.

Lastly, he placed the flute near his head with the crane's beak touching his cheek when he waited.

His last thought, through the throbbing of the leg, now swollen as large as a baby elephant's, was the story Grandfather had told him. The philosopher had asked the skull, "Surely you would grasp at a chance to return to your former life." His answer caused Man-Gee to smile, deep in the folds of his robe. "How can you think I would cast away joy greater than that of a king upon his throne," the skull asked, "only to go back to the toils of the living world?"

With his last breath, Man-Gee considered: A world to come when every season would be spring, and every sound the song of the love flute.

Part Two
The Voices

"What sound, this?"

Brave Dancer, the taller of two Indians, hesitated at the edge of the outcropping and considered the sound that had brought him to this place. He shifted hands and considered the rawhide thong loosely attached to a mottled red cow that trailed behind his horse. The strange wailing was a good omen, for it had brought him to this animal. The hide would make a fine robe, and the meat would feed the hungry children. He slid from the Appaloosa and crawled in a steady, cautious line toward the sound coming from inside the earth. His friend, Dog Tail, followed.

The white men had passed through the area the previous day on the trail the Lakota called "The Thieves Road," because it was built to steal their land. In passing, the longhair thieves had left behind their filthy camps and soiled dead. This time, however, they also left something useful, a healthy cow ready for the roasting fire. But this noise was not from a lost animal. Eerie and forbidding, it seemed to be neither of the white men nor of The People. Stealthily, they crept to the edge of the narrow gap and listened.

"Aieee," the other man whispered. "What comes of this moaning hole? It makes no *wasichu,* no white man's sound. Neither is it the wind that moans within the cavern. Nor the thunder, nor the bleating of a sheep or goat. Listen."

For long minutes they crouched, ready with their lances. A tiny ray of sunlight flickered into the cavern, but it stopped short of highlighting the cave floor. If there was a bottom to the fissure, the light did not bear witness. They could detect no movement, and no sound other than the strange-pitched wailing.

"Maybe *wanagi*, a ghost. We tell of this at council. Others must know."

With silent movements, they backed away and remounted, urging their horses and the cow toward their village.

Brave Dancer and Dog Tail tried to mimic the sound for the council, but their skills fell short of the task. The advisors agreed that they must travel to see for themselves this moaning hole.

Before the sun rose on the sleeping village, Brave Dancer was ready. He had already broken his fast with a handful of *wasna* and chilled water from the river, and even his Appaloosa pawed in anticipation. His sleep had been troubled because of a dream about the hole in the ground. In his dream, the crack widened and he saw what had taken residence in the earth. It was a spirit, wizened and tormented, with coarse, black hair like his own, but with eyes that were slanted, the corners exaggerated as he sometimes painted his own for battle. It did not walk upright like a man, but slid along the ground like a serpent, spewing anger and unhappiness. It would be best to treat the spirit with care, his dream told him. Perhaps an offering would appease it.

Brave Dancer returned to his teepee and chose two pieces of dried venison from the deerskin pouch that his wife had made. He rode proudly alongside the elders, sorry that the distance was not farther. The sun's rays scarcely licked the eastern plain when the five men crept through the dry grass, led by Brave Dancer. The elders took seats in a circle around the hole and he joined them.

The opening appeared much too small for any human to have descended through it. The chief made a motion with his hand to show that he agreed— no human dwelled in the ground. After a moment, he said, "The circle is complete. This is a good sign that the hole makes a circle, like the sun and the moon, like the trunk of a tree, this place is *wakan*, sacred." He moved his hand in a circular motion and returned to the opening. "But what sign comes from below? Not the growl of a beast. Has the spirit flown like a bird into the hole? Slithered like a serpent?" The others chuckled, and he added, "Maybe bats make their home below to frighten our warriors."

Brave Dancer felt his face heat with embarrassment, but what he had heard was not the sound of a bat. He was glad when one of the others spoke up. "Maybe it is an evil spirit waiting for one of us to die. A warning that the Crow will slay the enemy of our enemy?"

The chief scoffed. "What sound does this fierce beast make that our braves rush home to their women? I hear no sound. Maybe it is caused by dirty ears." He motioned impatiently. "Wake it up that we may hear."

When the spirit-creature failed to respond, Brave Dancer tossed a handful of pebbles through the opening while the men peered down, their lances ready to slash any apparition that drifted back up through the darkness. The pebbles bounced against the floor of the cavern, and soon the keening began as a weak, distracted whimper before building to a blood-curdling wail. Six heads drew back in surprise and not a little fear. The chief listened with great interest and began to imitate the sound.

From deep within the earth, the wailing intensified with an almost frantic quality. It seemed to Brave Dancer that the high-pitched strains sounded agonized. He brought forth a fire stick that he had carried from camp and tossed it down the hole. His fingers tightened around his lance, and he bent with the others to stare at the spot where the thin shaft of light pierced the darkness below. Suddenly the faint light caught a brief movement.

"Spirit moves," he whispered.

"Spirit-Who-Dwells-In-Darkness does not wish to be disturbed. Perhaps it is the *wanagi* of a great warrior who died without honor. *Wanagi* is angry because it does not rest." The chief spoke with great conviction. The others nodded, contemplating their own reaction if honorable death were denied them. Perhaps this great warrior had been hung like a dog by the white man. It was no wonder that this *wanagi* was filled with wrath. It would be good to appease it.

Brave Dancer tied a long thong of rawhide to the buffalo

bladder that held his drinking water and eased it through the opening. With the others watching, he lowered the thong as far as it would go, until he could extend his arm no further. When a tug reverberated up through the darkness and the bladder jerked from his hand, he withdrew so quickly that the others laughed. They would make a joke of him at council that night. Below, he heard the sound of slurping, like an animal that had gone many suns without drinking. The noise ceased and the wailing began again. He tossed two pieces of dried meat into the hole and heard the sound of scrambling, then silence.

"Spirit-Who-Dwells-In-Darkness is grateful. Let us return to the village and smoke the *chanunpa,* sacred pipe, over what we have seen here." The chief led the way back to a gnarled, lightning-split tree where the horses were tethered, while the cavern echoed with wailing as if from a dying buffalo calf.

The next day Brave Dancer returned with his first wife, Dons Blanket, and a Crow girl he had given her as a gift, after a triumphant battle in which he counted coup and brought back horses. The girl would ease his wife's burden, but only after she recovered from the scarring and tattooing that was proper for a slave. The girl remained behind the two of them as he showed Dons Blanket the hole. She withdrew a narrow deerskin thong from her packet and tied a dried gourd that she had filled with water. Inside she placed a handful of pemmican and watched as her husband lowered the gourd. When he withdrew his hand without the deer hide thong she had spent many hours chewing, she let out a grunt of disgust. The *wanagi* had kept her favorite gourd, one she had traded for a fat salmon to one of the southern tribes.

"You horse-piss ball of rabbit turd! Let your sweat fill your bladder from this day forward. I do not honor a demon warrior with my best pot," she shouted.

A wail of pain echoed up through the opening, causing the slave girl to crouch on her heels and sway from side-to-side, making no sound, even when Dons Blanket cupped her on the side of the head with her scraping stick. A moment later, she booted the girl, and they returned to the camp.

That night in the council, Brave Dancer told a story of *shunk-manitu*, Coyote, Iktome, spider-man, and Iya, the rock. In this story, the rock had power. Coyote took the blanket from his back and gave it to Iya to keep the rock from freezing. Later, when Coyote found himself in need of the blanket, he returned and grabbed it from Iya's mossy, spider-veined surface. "What is given is given," Iya protested, but Coyote thought only of his own misery. Later, Iya came seeking revenge for the theft of his blanket; thundering, rolling across the plains, crashing across water, smashing trees in his wake as Coyote and his friend, Iktome, tried to hide from its wrath. "What is given is given." Brave Dancer thought about the story, and knew that gifts were powerful things. Perhaps this spirit was Iya, the rock.

***

One of the warriors who had scoffed at the telling nodded. He had come to see for himself, this thing that dwelled in the ground.

The chief nodded. "It is as Brave Dancer describes."

The hunting party gathered around the hole and listened to the strange sounds coming from the hole where Spirit-Who-Lives-In-The-Darkness dwelled, crazed screams such as that of a scalded wild cat from the Black Hills, the sound soon joined by the sound of sticks clapping. The wail of an old woman in mourning drifted up, along with unearthly shrieks of a trapped animal. The Council was right; this Warrior Spirit must be appeased so that it would remain underground.

Leaping onto their horses, the four warriors circled the rock formation before galloping off in the direction of the river. Later that day they returned with a haunch of venison still attached to its roasting stick. One of the braves jumped from his horse and dropped the offering into the moaning hole. When he heard it clunk on the bottom, he turned and remounted, ignoring the screams that followed him.

"It was good, your gift to this spirit. Perhaps it is responsible for your good hunting. We will do likewise. It will be a good thing." The chief had invited the hunting party into his teepee to retell their adventures. In the firelight, as the pipe was passed and the story retold, the Spirit's shrieks took on a power of their own. In the retelling, they grew louder, more ghostly and threatening. Everyone agreed: It was good to make offering to this Spirit.

When Brave Dancer met Fox Runner from the trading tribe in the low mountain country, he motioned in sign language; *Warrior-Spirit Sleep Under Earth. Demand Many Things.* He pointed toward the distance, where the rocks could be seen against the setting sun. Fox Runner nodded in understanding. He would make a wide path on his way back to his camp to see for himself.

Fox Runner's story of the Warrior-Spirit was retold in his own camp and soon a trail led to the rocks where the Warrior-Spirit was entombed. The People brought gifts of frybread, *wojapi,* berry soup, and squash. One mother held her boy baby over the small opening in the hopes that the brave Warrior who dwelt beneath would infuse the budding brave with courage. She was rewarded with such strange, desperate shrieks that a shudder passed through her. It was determined that young women of the village would not be allowed near to protect the unborn children from the *wanagi's* wrath. The warriors appreciated the horrible fate that had dealt their comrade, and they gave great consideration to what the Warrior-Spirit might have done in his past life to bring such a punishment upon himself.

One day, the smell of smoke blew from the west, and soon after a line of fire drove the horses into a frenzy. The crier ran about, telling the women to take down their teepees. They pulled down the lodgepoles and folded their teepees into trim packs and lashed them on their horses and travois, with tent poles holding the packets and the small children, to keep them out of the way. The fire carriers stood in the river, holding burning fire sticks while the sky burned around them.

Some of the women were slow and could not finish in time, so they left their teepees standing, and their houses and possessions burned. Dons Blanket had her possessions scattered in the rush to stay ahead of the roaring fire. Later, when the camp was relocated a short distance away, she kicked her slave girl and made her help with the scraping of hides gathered too soon that now needed extra cleaning. Later, when she went to see what work had been done, one of the buffalo hides was missing. She cast a sharp glance at the slave, but the girl had her head down, working. Perhaps in the confusion, one of the other women had gathered what belonged to her. She would ask later.

Brave Dancer waited as Winged Pony rubbed bear grease on his burns. The people were lucky to have only lost a litter of puppies and one pony to the fire. The other livestock had been driven into the river and safety. He smiled at this second wife as she worked softly to avoid disturbing the reddened areas. Had she not been so efficient, so skilled in the way that she dismantled the teepee and packed their baskets and skins into dried hide boxes, they would have lost more. He had suffered burns when he retraced his steps to help his other wife. In the end, it had been for naught. Now he would bear the scars of his bravery. Winged Pony's shy admiration told him that it was a good thing.

"Wife, more water." His throat was scratched and raw from the smoke he had breathed. Even as he had raced back through the line of fire to the river with Dons Blanket, he tried to hold his breath, but still the smoke had seeped inside him like a fire made with wet wood on a windy night.

The buffalo had moved on. The advisors announced that the buffalo and the deer were many days ahead, where the fire had not destroyed the grasses. They too must follow. But before he left, he would pay one last visit to the Spirit-Who-Lives-In-Darkness. His people would not return to this land until the time of the new earth when the grasses and berries sprung anew from the fertile earth, bringing good feed for the buffalo.

From a distance, he saw that the fire had burned over the spot where the *wanagi* dwelled. The rock formation was as familiar as before; no fire could take the landmarks from the people. He had brought nothing to offer the spirit, for there was nothing to spare in his village. The spirit would have to go unappeased until times were better. Ahead, he saw an animal crouched at the opening where the spirit sounds came from the earth. A young wolf sniffed at the opening, oblivious to the presence of the Indian and his horse. Brave Dancer slipped down and crept closer. The wind was at his face, and the wolf did not sense danger. Whining like an excited camp dog digging for gophers, it sensed something within the darkness.

Brave Dancer drew his arrow and felt the sinews of the bow rub against his scalded arm, but the pain was nothing to a warrior. He kept the bow straight, and the arrow flew swiftly toward its target, brushing against the wolf's leg without penetrating, as he had intended. The young wolf half-hopped into the air, lost its footing and dropped into the hole. Brave Dancer crept closer.

Beneath the ground, he heard the sharp movements of a rattlesnake. What sort of spirit could turn itself into a serpent at will? Still, there was no denying the familiar rustle of rattles dancing in the darkness. Puzzled, he considered that the Warrior-Spirit's medicine might be more powerful than he had imagined. Perhaps this spirit was Turko, the rock god, dwelling in this place. Stooping, he took his knife, pried a portion of the stone that lay near the opening and added it to his medicine bag. He untied the water skin from the back of his horse and lowered it into the hole with his horsehair rope. Chanting his morning song to his ground spirits, he felt the rope jerked out of his hands. He had not meant to make the sacrifice of his best rope to the Warrior-Spirit, but the Spirit's medicine was more powerful than his own. He returned to camp and began to gather his horses for the long journey.

Some moons later, Brave Dancer was troubled by a dream that occurred three nights in a row. In his dream he was escaping the fire, traveling swiftly in order to reach fresh forage before the horses gave out. His wife, Winged Pony, rode behind with the other women, her papoose bound securely against her back. Dons Blanket was there as well. They passed many carcasses of animals that had fallen in the fire—the weak and injured, and the young who could not outrun the swift prairie fire. He glanced at a young buffalo calf that would have fed the entire tribe. As he rode, his keen eye caught a movement. The spirit walked upright, dark and furred like a bear, but it moved like no bear that he had ever seen. Curious, he let his horse pick its way toward the apparition until something caused the hair on his nape to rise.

The apparition seemed to be neither human nor animal. It walked with an ungainly limp, on two legs rather than four, but covered with a skin. Holding his lance, he urged his horse forward.

The Appaloosa shied at the smell of the pelt, a fine buffalo skin. Something else caught his attention: The water that swung lightly from the apparition's side was Dons Blanket's work. He glanced again and saw two eyes peering out from the pelt. His eyes were made clear, and he understood the vision in front of him. He recognized the approaching figure, its skin yellow but covered in red paint, with fire coming from its head. His gifts had freed the *wanagi* from its prison, and now it crept toward him with painful steps.

When it spoke, its words were strange, but not the ranting of an evil being. Haggard, starved, it showed much sign of having suffered. Its feet bled from the rocky ground, its hands were blistered and raw. Surely it had withstood great trial before the Great Spirit consented to free it. Beside him, the chief nodded his agreement. "It is he."

In his dream, the Spirit's face was hidden. Brave Dancer did not question this, for the ways of the Great One were not to be reckoned. He awakened, determined to share his dream with the medicine man, for the old one would know what he must do.

Before evening, scouts rode into camp with word that they had sighted the buffalo herd, a day's ride north in a big valley where the beasts had crossed the sweet water near the Big Horn. The criers went through camp telling the women to begin packing. Dons Blanket was in a foul mood because she could not Find the worthless Crow dog-slave who had slipped away when the work was done and did not return until the moon was in the middle of the sky. Brave Dancer shook his fist at his wife and reminded her that there was much to be done. He was hurrying away while she stood with her own fist raised around her skinning knife, shouting that he must find the slave girl and cut off her nose for running away. He ignored her command. The treatment of a slave was women's business.

The path to the *wanagi's* den had fresh tracks that did not match his own, the small and light tracks of a girl carrying water.

He followed and heard his first wife hurrying to catch up. This was not her concern, but he did not bother to upbraid her. Anger would spill off her tongue, and he was not in the mood to hear it. Ahead, he heard the faint, muffled sound of a love flute. At the top of the sacred circle where the people gathered to hear the *wanagi's* wailing, the slave girl sat with her head back, listening with her hands clasped over her breasts as though she were embracing her beloved. The breeze caught her singed hair, and he saw the remains of her mangled ear, a punishment for burning meat or spilling water one too many times for Dons Blanket to tolerate. But this night she sat with her back straight, her knees bent beneath her like a bride while the music sang of longing and love. It was a song that a brave would play for a maiden in the hidden grasses of the river while he worked up courage to tie horses before her teepee.

Brave Dancer halted. Perhaps this *wanagi* was a Crow dog, a cowardly boy who had run from battle instead of standing proudly with his leg tied to the ground so that he had no choice but to stand and fight. Or one of the Crows who hired out as a scout for the white man's army, tracking the Lakota for the longhairs. Whichever, the *wanagi* suffered its fate in the moaning hole. The girl would suffer as well, for Dons Blanket carried her skinning knife. A missing nose would be a warning to other slaves not to wander off in the dark.

When the girl turned and saw them, she gave a strange smile and stood. For a moment, he imagined her as a Lakota maiden and not a despised dog-slave. But the feeling passed. He grabbed her arm and began dragging her back to the camp.

Behind, the flute sounds halted. He turned, recalling the dream and half-expecting to see a spirit floating toward him, a vision with red painted body and fire bolts coming from his head. But it seemed that a puff of sacred breath floated out of the opening and merged with the night air. The girl twisted and saw it as well, for her eyes lit with joy.

Dons Blanket saw nothing but hate. "Hurry up, husband. You coddle this dog. She will pay for her disobedience with her life. There is no good to come from feeding a dog that keeps running away. Look at her. What kind of squaw does the Crow breed that does not know her place? I am better off with no one to scrape my hides and carry water. We should throw this dog in the hole with her *wanagi* warrior and be done with her."

Brave Dancer sighed. "Winged Pony will need help when the child comes. I will give you another gift."

He released the girl in front of Winged Pony's teepee with enough force to satisfy Dons Blanket. The slave girl went sprawling in the dirt. He straightened and started toward the river to ponder the things he had seen at the Warrior-Spirit's den. His first wife was still speaking, and his second had emerged from her teepee with her fist raised in anger.

Women! He had two wives, and yet he knew nothing of them. "You two settle it. *Hetchetualo.* It is so."

Suddenly the girl sprung to her feet and began running back in the direction of the *wanagi*. His wives glanced at each other and began running after the girl. Brave Dancer glanced to where his horse stood waiting, but he was in no mood. Instead, he started toward the group of men who were watching the women and joined their laughter. It was no concern of his what his wives did.

Still, the women's yelling provided an opportunity. One of his friends offered a calico mare as a wager that the girl would escape. He glanced at the swiftness of Winged Pony, already outdistancing Dons Blanket and narrowing the gap on the slave. He nodded. He would hate to lose his favorite mare, but there was little chance of that, for the fleetness of his young wife was well known. He led the others to their horses to see for themselves the outcome of their wagers. He trotted after the women, not even riding hard to close the distance.

His second wife was nearly upon the girl. She grabbed the slave's arm and tried to pull her to the ground, but the girl wrestled free. Suddenly, the wind caught her ragged hair and her torn garment, and her feet seemed to leave the earth. He stared, unsure of his vision as the slave girl flew through the air and landed at the base of the hole where the spirit dwelled in the darkness. His wives yelled, but their noise was swallowed by a fierce wind that whipped the sage around their heads and brought the thundercloud to the land in a whirl of dust and small pebbles that stung his face.

As though in a dream, the girl raised her arms high above her head and arched her back with her eyes closed, as though offering a prayer to the god of the underground. He urged his horse closer and saw the strange, victorious smile that wreathed the slave girl's face, making her seem as beautiful as his first wife on her wedding day. Then, with the blink of an eye, the girl was gone. He heard the muffled echo of her descent into the ground, then silence.

His horse came to a halt beside the hole. His eyes saw nothing except darkness. He felt the wind die down and the earth grow still, until the only sound was that of Dons Blanket huffing from exertion as she approached. His wives stood side-by-side, staring into the hole, waiting for something to happen, but the *wanagi* was silent. When other women approached, laughing and hooting at the loss of a slave, his wives started back. He turned to the young brave who had won the bet and nodded his assent. The brave had gained a fine mare. To lose both the slave girl and the horse in one day was a hard thing. Maybe the *wanagi* was the slave girl's Crow warrior, unhappy with his offerings. Better that they leave this place.

Part Three
The Road

Road graders and skip loaders crawled across the flat landscape like giant praying mantises, biting every hill in their path. Hank Barrows watched white smoke belch from the tall exhaust pipes of the oversized hoods, awed anew at the raw power of the machines. He glanced at the survey team half a mile ahead. Man, he wished he was with them instead of babysitting the walkie-talkie and portable radio inside his service truck. A water truck parked alongside a stretch of newly-graded road captured his attention.

"What the heck's that truck doing? Don't tell me we've got another breakdown. One more setback, I'll swear this place is jinxed." He reached for the radio to find out why the truck wasn't where it was supposed to be. "Jeff, looks like you're needed out here, pronto."

Hank replaced the speaker and slumped back against the seat, resting his head on the backrest. The building of a lousy road the Wyoming plains had been plagued with too many problems. Back at headquarters, the suits howled at the endless delays—and he had another eighteen miles to go.

His intercom buzzed again.

"Boss, we got something you gotta see," one of the surveyors said with a note of excitement in his voice.

Crumpling his soda can into a lump, Hank tossed it into the bed with the others, muttered a mild oath, and jerked his truck into gear, careful to slow at the approach so his dust wouldn't cover the group crouched in a semi-circle at the base of a rock outcropping. His stomach lurched when he noticed a ring of stones circling the hole. There was nothing good going to come out of this. Nothing.

"We got a problem," the surveyor repeated. "Lookie here."

Hank took the offered flashlight and pointed its light downward through a narrow shaft in the earth. His whistle was partly surprise, partly admiration. "What the blazes?" Dropping to his knees, he extended his arm and slowly rotated the beam. When he had seen enough, he straightened and turned to the man next to him.

"Something was living down there." The surveyor scratched his chin.

Hank removed his hat and wiped the sweat from his matted forehead. "Not something," he muttered. "Someone."

The men exchanged looks. Their teams had come across nothing in the area that suggested another opening, only this single shaft scarcely twelve inches across.

"Boss, maybe we better get a dump truck of cement over here, pronto. Get the thing filled in," the surveyor suggested, with a quick glance around at the others.

Hank was careful to keep his eyes on the opening while he considered his options. They all knew the stakes for tampering with relics in Indian territory, which was a federal crime. But he had to answer to headquarters. If he made the call to halt construction, even for a few hours, the bean counters would nail his hide to the corporate wall. Like they said at the Indian casino down the road, he had just hit the jackpot, only this one was a no-winner.

Seconds ticked by while he stared into the cavern. Finally, his integrity won out. To heck with the company. He'd rather catch hell for the right decision than destroy something irreplaceable. He rocked back on his heels. "I'll put in a call to Red Cloud."

By late afternoon, he followed the faded blue of John Red Cloud's ancient GMC pickup across the valley floor, choking on dust as the Lakota tribal observer screeched to a stop, just inches from Hank's back bumper.

"Good to see you." Hank held out his hand, relieved that the man was alone.

Red Cloud met his handshake with a knuckle-crushing grip. "Yeah, sure. What's going on? Wife said you sounded like you'd been in the sun too long."

"Something like that." The sight of a white vehicle approaching from the same direction Red Cloud had just come made Hank yank off his cowboy hat. "How'd you suppose they got wind of this?" He waited, but Red Cloud stood in silence. He took a deep breath. "We got us a problem."

Red Cloud eyed the approaching vehicle's dust. "You better make this quick, Road Builder. That university archeologist and his crew will be here in about five minutes."

Hank nodded. "I'm not sure what we got here, might be an Indian ruin, a burial cave, or the den of a confused prairie dog. Whatever it is, I don't aim to share it with that crew." He led the way to the shaft.

He handed Red Cloud a flashlight and waited while the other man flattened himself onto the dust and repeated Hank's sweeping scan of the cavern. When Red Cloud rose to his knees, he snapped the light off and remained still.

"Any ideas?" Hank turned from watching the dust approaching from the east to the construction crew pushing the road toward them from the north.

Red Cloud nodded. "I have heard the old ones speak of a Warrior Spirit—"

"Say what? You mean we got us a ghost?" Hank wasn't sure who took jurisdiction over ghosts.

"*Wanagi* is no ghost. Not exactly. It's a . . . to my people, it's special. A warrior spirit. They say one lives in this place."

Hank flickered a glance at Red Cloud then turned back to the earth movers puffing down the road a few miles back. "What's that mean for us?"

Red Cloud gestured toward the wide plains. When he spoke, his voice was filled with anger. "It means you make a bend in your road. There are things we cannot explain. But you will not touch the cave."

It was Hank's turn for anger. Too much depended on him to get this project done and soon. "Now wait a cockeyed minute. You better have a darn good reason because I'm not falling for some ghost story."

"No road passes near this cavern. No road!" Red Cloud started back to his pickup, his cell phone in his hand.

Hank watched. In an hour, half the reservation would be camped out along his survey line. Stifling his anger, he stalked to the driver's side and rapped on the window. "Wait a minute. Let's settle this thing tonight. In town?"

Red Cloud tossed his phone on the bench seat and powered down the window. Behind them, Trevor Benson, the archeologist from the university, pulled up in a state-issued Suburban with half a dozen graduate students in the seats. The two men watched as they descended with notebooks and enough field gear to hold up the project for a month.

Hank motioned toward their pickups and murmured for Red Cloud's ears only, "I'll put the university people off. No access until we know what we're looking at. Milly's Restaurant?"

Red Cloud grunted his approval and waited in the truck while Hank sauntered over to the archeologist to explain that they had made the long trip for nothing. He promised to notify them if the road crew turned up anything of scientific value. He remained in the partially completed roadway until the van disappeared over the hill, headed toward another site. On his way to check on the broken water truck, he saw Red Cloud still at the cavern with his big flashlight.

***

At seven o'clock, Red Cloud walked into the restaurant. Hank waited while he pulled out a chair and slumped into it. A waitress arrived to take their orders for two beers and an order of wings. When the drinks arrived, Hank occupied himself with pouring his drink into a cold frosted glass. Red Cloud toyed with the foam dripping off his beer as if his bottle was the only thing on his mind. When the waitress disappeared, Hank glanced around to assure himself that no one was within hearing.

"Do we have a problem?" Whatever happened, it would be less of a problem with Red Cloud than half a dozen other tribal observers Hank had worked with on previous assignments. Red Cloud was a fair man, devoted to the tribe with the same passion Hank saved for roads.

"Uh-huh." Red Cloud drummed the tabletop with his thumb.

"So talk." Hank took a swig of his drink.

"About a hundred fifty years ago, my great-great grandfather, a warrior called Brave Dancer, found a cave . . ."

Hank picked up a wing and dipped it into a dollop of ranch dressing as Red Cloud shared the story that had been passed down from father to son and finally to Red Cloud himself, a tale about offerings, prayers, and the keening sound of a Warrior-Spirit in a moaning cave. If it were true, then that cave was, as Red Cloud said, a sacred place. Hank watched Red Cloud's eyes for a sign that the story might be a tribal tale someone had invented for gullible white tourists, but he saw only intensity in the other's expression. If it were a hoax, then Red Cloud was the best storyteller in the Lakota nation.

The waitress arrived with another round. Hank poured his fresh beer into the glass while Red Cloud continued his story. Several long moments passed after Red Cloud finished speaking. Finally, Hank roused himself to the business at hand. "I'll need something concrete to go on."

"You have the story. From the Old Ones." Red Cloud folded his arms across his chest.

"Come on, you know that's not enough. Give me something else." Hank met the other man's eyes straight on.

"Ain't nothing. I'm saying it's enough."

Hank rubbed his thumb on the edge of his mustache. There was only one way to find out if the story was true. "Let's open it up."

"No!" Red Cloud pounded the table with his fist.

"Confound it, if it was a spirit, there wouldn't be anything there. You saw what was down there. That was no ghost."

Red Cloud hesitated.

Hank imagined the other man's college training colliding with his great-great-grandfather's memory. In the end, curiosity won out for the truth.

"When?"

"No time like the present. Let's see what we're talking about before we call in the cavalry." Hank could feel the excitement growing inside his belly like they were kids on a midnight caper. "Let's take my truck."

***

Hank aimed his headlights on the opening, then put the truck into park. A breeze from the south tempered the hot summer night. A coyote halted to watch them. The moon overhead lit the ground, and a million stars sprinkled the inky-black sky, the same view that someone trapped beneath the earth would have seen from the manhole at their feet. Hank's throat tightened as he pulled a couple of shovels from the truck bed.

He pitched his voice low, even though there was no one around to hear. "I'll tell you one thing, if it wasn't a spirit, I don't know what it was. Only a kid would fit through that hole."

Red Cloud remained silent while they enlarged the opening. Finally, he set his shovel aside. "This is big enough. How you plan to get down there?"

"I'll tie a rope to my bumper." Hank eyed his companion. "You an army man?"

"Marines."

"Close enough. We probably trained with the same ropes. I'll go first." Hank secured a rope to his truck's bumper, then swung his feet over the ledge, turning so he could rappel down the sides of the cave wall once he cleared the opening. He tied a flashlight pointing down on his belt and pushed off, dropping down quickly. As soon as he touched rock at the bottom, he moved aside as Red Cloud descended. Back-to-back in the center of the small natural cave, they trained their lights around the perimeter, sweeping up and down the perpendicular walls.

"Don't see another way out. How about you?" Hank asked.

Red Cloud merely grunted.

The smooth walls held no indentations to indicate a way out. Hank's light picked up a pile off to the side. "Look at this." His voice bounced off the walls, emitting an almost ghostly sound. What would someone listening at the opening think to hear that?

Red Cloud's flashlight beam joined his.

Hank almost didn't want to ask, but curiosity got the better of him. "What is it?"

Red Cloud bent close to the pile, then straightened. "Animal bones, mostly cooked. Roasted over a fire. See how the ends are blackened? Some are venison. Some smaller. Some big. Buffalo. Maybe bear."

Hank stared at the old bones. "What does it mean?"

"My people say the Spirit Warrior ate them." Red Cloud's voice had a strange timber to it.

Hank moved his light away from the bones. Three gourds sat lined up along the wall. One still had a stiff leather thong attached to a bladder skin that was so brittle it broke at the touch of Hank's boot tip. "I'll be foxed. Water jugs."

His flashlight picked up a place along the wall where the rock gave way to dirt, and what appeared to be the dried-up remains of a tiny gully. "Look at this—a water channel." The beam of light picked up no moisture in the cave. Something must have happened to divert the ground water.

"The dam," Red Cloud said, his voice soft but sure. "When you whites put it in, about eighty, eighty-five years ago, it dried up a lot of underground streams for our people."

Next to the bones lay a pile of worn rags and skins. "Looks like someone got their use from these." Hank poked at the squares of buckskin, or what remained of it, atop a piece of homespun fabric. He unfolded it. "What the—? It's a kid's shirt. A little kid's."

The shirt was barely held together, but the shoulder seams were intact, along with one sleeve, and enough of a front to see that it hadn't been worn by a Warrior Spirit.

Something dropped to the side when he unfolded the shirt, and Red Cloud stooped to retrieve it. "An arrowhead. Obsidian.

It's got Lakota markings. Maybe Brave Dancer's." Next to it was a tiny tooth, so chalky and fragile that Red Cloud left it laying where it rested in a scrap of deerskin. "It's a molar."

The ray from Hank's flashlight shook slightly as he stared at it.

A low crevice in the wall contained what appeared to be religious statues. Hank focused his light on the statues. "These are pagodas or something. Oriental. I've seen these things in a museum once. Asians carve them to honor their relatives."

Red Cloud squatted and examined one closely without touching it. "That seems strange to you?"

Hank ignored him. "Looks like it was an altar. They're all along here. Must be twenty of them. Will you look at the detail!" The calcium had deteriorated until the bones looked like they would fall into dust if someone blew on them.

"Look at this." Red Cloud's voice held a note of urgency. Hank joined his flashlight beam with Red Cloud's on a small buffalo rug. Red Cloud carefully reached out with his boot and flipped a corner over. Another tap and the rug unfolded.

Hank moved closer, his ragged breath joining Red Cloud's. Their lights flooded the rug like two halves of the same beam, never wandering from the two tiny skeletons dwarfed by the pelt. "It's a couple of kids."

"The one on the right looks like a girl. Look, her skull is crushed. At least she didn't suffer." Red Cloud stood without moving.

Hank's own eyes had tears in them as they tried to assimilate the sight in front of them. Their light beams swept across the small finger bones and the diminutive skulls resting above rib bones on the pelt. Nothing had been disturbed. The skeletons lay touching with the left one's arm wrapped around the girl in an embrace as though he had died protecting her. His body lay curled into a ball like a fetus in the womb.

Red Cloud nudged Hank, pointing to the right thigh, where a fracture had never healed.

"He must have fallen in here and couldn't get out with that leg, poor devil." Hank shivered as the silence continued and the cave's cool air grew colder. He clicked off his own flashlight. "Kill the light for a minute."

In the pitch blackness, the cave seemed alive with waiting monsters. Hank snapped his light back on. "A kid alone in this darkness . . ." He didn't care that Red Cloud witnessed his shudder. After all, it was Red Cloud's ancestor who had stood atop the cave giving offerings to the spirit within. Why had they not recognized the cries for help? Not even a white child would be left in this hole.

"The Lakota are kind to children. My ancestors would have welcomed him into their tribe. Perhaps Brave Dancer would have adopted him."

"What happened?" Hank asked. "Do you think the kid was mute?"

Red Cloud shook his head. "No. There were stories of strange keening. He was not slow-witted to have survived so many weeks."

Their flashlights illuminated the strange carvings, arranged almost like an altar against the rock wall. Red Cloud pointed to the broken flute hidden beneath the rib bones. "It is a love flute, like the one my grandfather used to court my grandmother." The instrument's head bent gracefully in the shape of a crane. "I have seen these, but never as a kid's toy." The decoration and workmanship showed it was held in high esteem by the maker.

"Someone showed the kid how to play it. Look at how the holes are worn from hours of use," Hank whispered. The boy had something to occupy himself; somehow that made the imprisonment more bearable in Hank's mind. He turned to a carving of an Indian girl laying next to the flute. The details were stylized, the perfection of a lover's imagination.

"Hank, maybe this wasn't a child. I seen Viet Cong in 'Nam the size of a kid, but maybe eighteen, nineteen years old." Red Cloud picked up one of the carvings and set it down again. "This boy could have been one of the Chinese who came to build the railroads. He must have had a girlfriend up-top. She kept him alive. My great-grandfather thought he was a *wanagi*. Everyone was afraid of him but this girl. I wonder what happened to her?"

Hank stared at the second skeleton. "Looks like she decided

to join him. Makes as much sense as anything else."

"If he spoke in Chinese, my people wouldn't understand his words."

"Look at that, though." Hank pointed to the flute. "He had everything he needed. Even love. Maybe he *was* a *wanagi* and he called her down to him."

"If so, she died happy." Red Cloud shifted. "We need to leave," he growled. "This isn't our place."

The rope dangled from the shaft's opening eighteen feet up. Above that, a lonely crescent sliver of moon along with a million stars just out of reach. Suddenly, Hank understood Red Cloud's reluctance to intrude on this sacred place. Stuffing the flashlight in his waistband, he pulled himself up, using his feet to anchor his legs against the rope. Without his feet, without the strength of his thighs and calves, he would be powerless to get out of the cave. He blanked the thought from his mind and finished climbing. He was shaky with relief when he reached the open plain and the illuminating headlights of his truck. Seconds later, Red Cloud appeared.

Hank rested against the bumper. Fishing a cigarette from an old pack he had tossed in the glove compartment when he quit for the last time, months before, he offered one to Red Cloud and was surprised when he took it. His cigarette was nearly gone when he spoke. "What are we going to do about this?"

"Well," Red Cloud's voice was low-pitched. "Reckon it's your road."

Hank smiled at Red Cloud's obvious attempt to test him. "Reckon it's your Warrior-Spirit." They finished their smokes, tamped the butts into the sand with their boot tips and watched a falling star blaze across the darkness. "There any law says we have to report this?"

"Probably. White man's got a law for everything."

"You went to college. Ever read the law?"

"Nope."

"Me either." Hank continued to study the sky. "Can't break a law 'less you aim to."

"That a fact?"

Hank shrugged, then dragged a piece of sheet steel from the bed of his truck that more than fit the enlarged opening. Red Cloud helped him dig back far enough to fit the sheet nice and snug against the earth. Then the two of them piled earth to cover it. When they were through, five feet of good Wyoming dirt sealed off the cavern. Hank took one last look at the now-concealed cavern before climbing into his truck. Red Cloud climbed in beside him.

"Reckon my crew will run a transom around that rock outcropping. Soil's unstable." Hank started the engine and put the truck in reverse. "Maybe dangerous if a car struck it in a snowstorm. That's what I'll put in my report." He glanced over to where Red Cloud sat slumped against the window, looking out at the blackness as if it were speaking to him. For the next fifteen miles, the other man never moved.

***

Hank looked up as the battered GMC made its way toward the broken-down water truck he was working on. He wasn't surprised when Red Cloud stepped out and joined him. He wiped his greasy hands on a rag and offered his handshake. "What brings you out this way?"

"Came to see the detour. Heard in town you had to make a new cut." Red Cloud's expression didn't give away his thoughts.

"Found some unstable ground. Limestone deposits." Hank squinted into the setting sun. "Road's shaping up, don't you think?"

Red Cloud allowed a grin to flit across his face. "Good enough for a white man's road, I guess. Hey, I got something for you." He fished a piece of paper from his pocket and held it out to Hank.

Smoothing the crumpled paper, Hank read the date of the top, *September 24, 1856*, and the name of a newspaper. Underneath was a brief notice: *Reward of $2 offered for a run-away indentured servant, a Chinese boy, 14, named Man-Gee. Last seen early August in Wyoming territory, three days ride from the Big Sandy. Contact Orvis Whettmeyer, Oregon City.*

Hank finished reading and looked up to see John Red Cloud's eyes, which were almost black under the shadow of his cowboy hat. Hank blew out a breath. "You saw the statues, the altar. That kid forgave everything before he died. He died a warrior."

Red Cloud studied the paving machine as it rolled out a black sheet of hot asphalt, creating a layer of new heat waves with the stench of tar. "How long you figuring to be here?"

Hank snorted. "Anxious to get rid of us?"

"Asphalt brings more people."

Hank frowned at the old argument. "Also brings tourist money. Can't fight progress. Not like we live in a cave—" He winced until he saw his friend's exaggerated shake of disgust. "Hey—I'll see you at the restaurant tonight. Same time?"

Red Cloud drove off in a cloud of red dust that gave truth to his name, leaving Hank to contemplate the road ahead. The highway would be finished in three days. They'd done a good job, right on time, and no major problems. But before he started the next job, he'd be putting in for a new water truck.

As he turned to go, the wind caught his hat and sailed it across the prairie. He swore under his breath and took off after it, feeling like an idiot as he crow-hopped clumps of sage and buffalo grass. It occurred to him that he ought to keep an eye out for rattlers or he'd have more than a lost hat to worry about. From the southwest, a funnel cloud barreled toward him, whipping up the earth in a whirl of dust, branches, and sage. Not a funnel cloud because there was no rain. More likely a tornado. Out here? He folded his elbow up to shield his eyes and watched the wind pull good Wyoming soil out from under his feet like all the demons of hell were unleashed on him. In the silence, he heard the air filling with a sound, like a whistle.

No time to grab his phone to record the funnel. No one would believe him anyway—this one was just for him. He stood motionless as the funnel danced past the spot where his truck was parked, circled around the top of the cave, and picked up some of the dirt that he and Red Cloud had laid down over the hole. The sound of a flute pierced the air, playing a series of notes like something he'd heard in the plaza from a guy playing for tips. A sign at his feet had said he was playing an authentic love song. A warrior's love flute played to woo a maiden.

A few seconds later, the sound and wind disappeared, leaving the desert silent. He stood alone on the prairie, watching Red Cloud's truck disappear over the ridge. His crew was gone as well, headed back to town after a long day. In the silence, he felt a presence.

But what would he tell Red Cloud—that he'd met the Indian maiden? Or maybe the *wanagi?* He lifted his head and made a deep bow.

"Rest well, you two. Let the wind play your song for all eternity."

Lightning Source UK Ltd.
Milton Keynes UK
UKHW012026280121
377836UK00002B/71